Academy Nowhere

Zak Lettercast

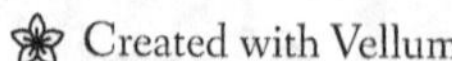 Created with Vellum

Dedicated to...

... T Van Santana, for beta reading the awful original version of this story and still being nice to me. You're a saint. I'm sorry we lost touch but your critiques quite literally changed my life.
... and to Ty Jacobo for being my friend for even longer than the first draft of this story sat untouched in a Google Drive folder.

Foreword

Hello, dear reader! I'm Zak Lettercast, and this is my short story, Academy Nowhere.

Academy Nowhere is originally published in the Story Den Publications Anthology titled "Distant Tales." I have secured permission to generate a limited number copies of my short story so that I can provide signed copies to my biggest fans. These are only intended to be gifts for my biggest fans (and promotional material for Story Den's thriller anthology series, should they desire it) and are therefore <u>not for sale</u>.

If you find yourself in possession of this very exclusive printed copy, you have either been gifted with or haplessly stumbled upon a rare gem. This item cannot be purchased anywhere online — you must be directly connected to me in some way in order to acquire one! Every copy that is available is hand-signed with a wet signature by yours truly.

I truly hope you enjoy this story and I hope you're inspired to read more work by me. See the last few pages for reading suggestions.

Thank you so much for being awesome.

Signed (quite literally)

Zak Lettercast
21 February 2024

Chapter One: Convenient Fondness

The battle between the territories had torn the world to shreds. Alliances had been made and broken, cities and countries overtaken, new boundaries forged. The realm would never be the same. But out of the chaos came regrowth. It was slow and flawed, but slowly humanity began to rebuild. Eventually, the West Desert birthed Beatrice Vermains.

The Vermains family were farmers, like most people in the quiet region. West Desert was hostile but livable. Her Nana was a technician during the war, so Beatrice was lucky enough to have access to some of the precious, ancient technologies that were mostly destroyed during the war. Technology-busting weapons had rendered most old-world tech useless and unfixable, and dampeners remained embedded in the terraformed earth, hindering the use of any communications devices.

Still, Beatrice's Nana, her namesake, had managed to save an old cellphone. It served as equal parts nostalgia monger and hope stirrer, pulled out at dinner time to tell Bea and her younger brother Maddeus all about life in the times before the war. Sometimes, Bea would sneak out with the cell phone and share it with her best friend, Dei. They would lay out under the naked night sky and make plans to run away into the past and live the lives they always dreamed of, fantastical lives full of mind-bending technology and hope for a better future.

Tonight was one of those nights. Beatrice held the glowing phone, with its cracked screen and errant haptics, over her face as she and Dei lay side by side in the dusty sand. They reached the part of Nana's electronic photo album that held her wedding pictures. Beatrice, now twenty-one years of age, had yet to find what her parents called a "proper suitor." Dei, who was also in his twenties, came from a poor family and was never expected to marry.

"I don't think I ever want to get married," Bea said as they scrolled through the old photos.

Dei silently wished he could have the privilege to say such a thing. Instead, he turned his head and studied how Bea's cheeks glowed in the dimming light of the phone screen. He imagined what she might look like in Nana's old wedding gown. "You'll have to, someday." He couldn't curtail the remorse in his voice.

She sat up on her elbow and looked down at him. Her face was so close to his. He could just sit up and kiss her right now if he wanted to. He wanted to. The spring air wafted around them for a moment, and an errant strand of her hair brushed his cheek, beckoning him near. He didn't move.

She smiled, an idea crossing her mind. "Will you marry me, Dei?"

Dei looked at her, baffled. "Don't joke about something serious like that," he said. His heart was racing. He hoped she couldn't hear it beating out its anxious drumline in his chest.

"I don't think I'm joking," she said, eyes wide with realization.

"Why would we get married?" He hoped it was because Bea had suddenly developed romantic feelings for him. He knew that was not the case.

"Why wouldn't we? I don't want to be married, but I have to. You're my best friend in the world, and I have never seen you so much as consider marrying anyone. We could just do it to get it over with and move on with our lives."

Dei didn't like the idea of her marrying anyone out of obligation. But he did like the general idea of her marrying him. Maybe she'd come to love him over time, that deep, fond, caring sort of love that grows like moss on old couples. And then he remembered something she said to him back when they were little kids just learning how to dig wells in the scrublands outside of town.

Her voice came like a soft canyon wind echo through his mind. "One of these days, I'm going to run away. Don't worry; I'll take you with me. Life without you wouldn't be life at all."

Bea studied his ponderous face for a few silent moments before getting up. "Forget it; it's a stupid idea." Sand fell from her clothes and onto his face as she turned to leave. He stood up to stop her, ignoring the grains that tickled the tip of his nose.

"I accept!" He said, the words tumbling out of him haphazardly as he tripped over his own feet to chase after her.

"What?" She laughed.

"I accept your proposal, Beatrice Vermains. I will become your husband."

"Seriously?"

He nodded. "Life without you wouldn't be life at all. How are we supposed to leave this damn place if you marry some washed-out hometown hero? You'd be stuck here forever, which means I'd be stuck here forever. That simply cannot happen. So, as weird as it sounds, I accept your proposal of a marriage of convenience."

Bea was laughing now, giggling into her shirtsleeve. The sand in her black hair looked like specks of stardust in the moonlight. Dei reached for her hand and pulled her close. She fell into his familiar embrace, then said something into his shoulder that he couldn't quite hear.

After a moment, she pulled back and looked up at him, beaming. "I've never wanted to get married before, but I've always wanted to plan a wedding."

Her lips were right there, just inches away from his. He could kiss her now if he really wanted to. He really wanted to. He did nothing.

Chapter Two: Happily Never After

"I always knew you two would end up together!" Nana said above the general festive noise of the wedding. It had been three weeks since the convenient proposal, and the entire village, all the Vermainses, and all the Lorituses had all come together in eager celebration.

The ceremony was short and simple, as they often were in those times. Weddings were always spiritual affairs, binding the two souls together for eternity while also intertwining the destinies of each represented family. The betrothed pledged their lives to each other, and the families formed alliances to safeguard their legacies. It was always sealed with a kiss.

This particular event was nothing special, but in it, Hodei Loritus and Beatrice Vermains both found memories worth cherishing for a lifetime.

For Dei, it was the way Bea looked in her off-white gown. It was a large, poofy thing that would have looked utterly ridiculous under any other circumstances. But today, with her dark hair framing her face in perfect ringlet curls, and the bright red of her painted toenails standing out against the billowing dust as she walked toward him, she was the embodiment of perfection.

For Bea, it was the way Dei looked at her as she approached him at the altar. He had always looked at her with a little something extra behind his gaze. Now that something extra was overflowing and all-consuming. At first, she recognized it as fondness. Only when they shared their first kiss in front of all those witnesses did she understand it as deep, unrelenting love.

All those years he had spent by her side, all the smiles and starry skies, and it had taken such a bold action for her to see things the way they truly were. As his lips pressed into hers and their eternal fate was sealed, she found herself alone with him, in their own private world, far, far away from West Desert. The words she said to him so long ago rang through her mind, and she decided to take their fate into her own hands.

They were going to run away from West Desert.

She told him so that night as they lay together in the wedding tent at the village center, whispered it into his ear like the most sacred secret she could ever possibly impart. The villagers' revelry had not died down, though the grayest edges of the sun's rays were beginning to peek up from the horizon. The sky would be alight with the fiery hues of desert dawn in just an hour or so.

He ran his hand down her arm, fingertips grazing her skin with impossible gentleness. "West Desert is all we've ever known," he said, "and as a man of little means, I can't make your dream come true alone."

She smiled, cupping his cheek in her hand. The gesture was unfamiliar and somewhat awkward but pleasant in its newness. Butterflies and possibility fluttered inside her chest. Butterflies, and potential, and something else. Not love. Not like how he loved her. No, this something was tainted with a hint of a sour kind of sadness, of vacancy. Gritty, it was a sandstorm in her gut, threatening to suffocate the joy making its nest in her. She pushed it down. She focused on their future together, someplace away from the dust.

"I can make it happen for both of us." She leaned in and kissed him. Sweetness mixed between them until they could not hold themselves back from falling beneath the covers together for the third time that night. Her sandstorm was all but forgotten.

Dawn crept in, silently at first. The entire town was hungover. The newlyweds' off-white tent glowed bright yellow as the sun made its ascent in the sky. Beatrice awoke to the beautiful sound of Dei's sleepy breath beside her.

And then their world shattered to pieces.

At first, the noise sounded like cattle being herded. There was a low rumble and shouts from men in the distance. Bea watched as Dei darted awake and glanced around when the low rumble began to shake the ground entirely and overshadow the shouts.

Quickly, the pair got dressed and ran outside their tent. Dei's pants and boots were unfastened, Bea's shirt and pants were disheveled, but they made it out of the structure just in time to see it collapse in on itself from the shaking. A million possibilities darted through the minds of the villagers as they collected, groggy, around the well at the town's center.

"Stampede?" Some shouted, but no cattle could be seen. Glasses toppled and rolled off tables, dumping red wine into the dirt like blood.

"Earthquake?" Others murmured as dust began to rise in ominous clouds around them.

"Sinkhole?" One cried as the crowd began to panic, many unable to keep their footing, most frantic to find their loved ones.

Suddenly, the rumbling stopped. Dust hung in the air like curtains. The villagers' screams lowered to an anxious murmur.

"Is it over?" Dei asked.

That's when the shooting started.

Chapter Three: Blood is Thick

Bright blue lasers pierced the brown clouds that shrouded them. Dead bodies hit the ground before anyone could scream. Chaos ensued. Bea froze as a laser shot the man beside her. She looked into his eyes as he lay there, thinking that he looked familiar somehow. Those brown eyes, cloudy and wet. That face contorted in a final moment of pain and terror. Those fingers covered in blood and clutching at the melon-sized hole in his torso.

Dei grabbed Bea's arm and dragged her through the swirling mass of bodies away from where the lasers had come. She stared at the man, trying to remember how she knew him. A woman fell to her knees beside him, her elegant dress soaking up the man's ichor from the too-parched earth.

"Palmer!" The woman was sobbing now. Bea could hear her over the ambient screaming and stampeding of the crowd. The voice was unmistakably her mother's, though the withering figure seemed too frail, too primal to be the unstoppable Louisa Vermains.

But it was Louisa. And Palmer, the man Bea had

watched die before he hit the ground, was her father. But he could not be her father anymore because he was dead. Her mother followed him shortly after Bea's view was cut off as Dei led her into an alleyway between the adobe buildings. Her brother and Nana were nowhere to be found.

For a moment, things were quiet as they ran through the deserted labyrinth. The screams and the cold hum of laser canons faded to distant whispers of war. Bea wanted to stop. She wanted to throw up. She wanted to cry.

"Dei, please, let's rest a moment, please–"

Dei chose not to hear her. "They're coming, Bea. You know what this is. We have to get out of here before it's too late. Keep going." He breathed hard between the words, throat and lungs burning from dusty morning air and the wave of smoke quickly catching up to them.

"They're dying out there! My father–" a sob choked in her throat.

"We can't save them, but we can save ourselves. You said we'd run away, right? Leave West Desert?"

Bea didn't respond. The edge of her vision was going gray.

"Live up to your promise, Bea. Let's run away together. Right now."

They rounded the final corner in the dense cluster of buildings as he said it. The dirt street opened up before them, eerily empty, houses shuttered. A baby cried in the distance. If she tried hard enough, Bea could imagine the sounds emanating from the town center were a continuation of the wedding reception revelry. Two more miles to home.

They raced through yards and hopped fences. The sun rose higher, and sweat percolated on their skin. Bea's lips were dry and cracked. She'd only had wine the night before, and it wasn't sitting well in her gut. The Vermains farm-house was in sight now, sitting proud by the big old mesquite. Bea's legs burned with acid, lungs squeezing hard and fast for air.

"I'm not going to make it," she said, knees turning to jelly, vision fading fast.

"We're close, Bea. Keep moving," Dei said, pulling her hard now.

"I can't see...."

"Follow my voice. You can rest when we get inside."

"Inside?" She felt the darkness taking her, like smoke clouding her sight and throat.

"Yes, Bea. Inside. Just a few more steps now, and you can rest while I pack us a bag." And everything went dark.

The sting of tearing skin and the taste of iron catapulted her into wakefulness. Her vision filled the town burning, black smoke boiling up like soup in a pot, bodies cooking under the blue laser fire. Her ears thrummed with the sound of rushing blood. Dei leaned over her. He was saying something, mouth and eyes equally wide with urgency and fear.

"Huh?" She sat up. Her head swum. She twisted to the side, stomach revolting against her anxious, dry swallow. The ground shook with the thundering steps of a distant machine giant, framed by smoke, visible in all its terrible glory from the porch steps of the Vermains farmhouse. Small aircraft buzzed like fleas around the mechanical beast. It was something out of a nightmare. It was impossible. It was happening.

"I'm going to grab our things," Dei said, voice ragged and breathy. "If you need me, yell." His face was beet red, forehead beading with sweat.

Bea was still gathering her bearings when the screen

door closed behind him. She looked down at her exposed arms, where the skin had peeled away from dragging on the sandpaper earth. Dei had evidently pulled her all this way from somewhere down the road. The dirt sealed her wounds, coloring her dried blood a decidedly ominous green-black.

Bea suddenly realized she was very, very thirsty. Her mouth was full of acid and dirt, and she hadn't had water or small beer in almost a full day. Dei would know to bring water, but she felt the need to remind him anyway. She twisted around to call to him through the screen door, but when she opened her mouth to yell, nothing came out. Her voice was gone, vocal cords rubbed raw by the soot and sand.

There came a sound from the sky then, a sort of whistling sizzle. She stood, wobbly on jelly legs, and made her way out from beneath the porch. The air was orange now, dense smoke blotting out the sun's light. She shielded her eyes against its dim glare and noticed two – no, three – specks of blue-green light streaking the sky like falling stars.

Smoke trailed the stars, white-gray against the dark, late-morning sky. For a moment, she thought only two of them were moving until she realized that one of the glimmering specks was getting bigger and bigger, louder, and louder. It was not a shooting star.

"Dei!" She called out to her lover in the house. But her voice was stale and dry, like dead leaves rustling in an autumn breeze. "Dei!" she tried again. The glowing ball of blue-green fire was heating the ground now as it sped toward her at an ungodly rate. The whistling sizzle was the sound of an angry hornet's nest now, nearly drowning her out when, for the third time, she called out her lover's name, and her voice broke through the parched dirt that caked up her throat. "Dei!"

But it was all she could say before she took off running again, racing for her life against the missile that was hurtling toward her home and her husband and everything she had ever known. Terror struck her for the first time that day when one of the other missiles made contact across the valley, and the shockwave rattled her bones. She ran harder, faster. She practically flew, clumsy limbs a blur of frantic effort as she strove to put as much distance between her and the harbinger of death that was bearing down on her from above.

The missile tapped the ground, and, for a moment, time stood still. She heard the click of the detonator and then – nothingness. Her vision filled with bright white light, and the smell of incineration overcame her. She was knocked to the ground and pummeled by the blastwave, even as she took shelter behind the schoolhouse where she and Dei had spent their early youth.

Covered in rubble and so painfully disoriented, she submitted herself to death.

Chapter Four: Reborn

"This one's alive," came a flat, clinical voice. A flashlight shone sharply in Bea's eyes.

No, she thought, I'm dead. I'm dead, and this is hell.

The light came off her face, and she blinked into the darkness. She tried to move, but nothing responded. The faces staring down at her were blank, masked things wearing blue and white shrouds. She could see her reflection in them, bluish and bruised. She opened her mouth to speak, but nothing came out – just like when she had tried to warn Dei.

A warm tear spilled from her eye.

"Is it viable?" One of the faceless beings asked.

"Affirmative. The body is severely mangled, but the mind is intact."

"Good. The Beastmaster can rebuild it to the Prince's needs, blessed may they be."

Beastmaster? Prince?

As far as Bea was concerned, this was all the delusional concoction of her dying mind. It was all too fantastical, too painful to be real. She closed her eyes and rested for a while, waking up periodically as her maimed body traveled from the schoolhouse, through ruins, over and around the dead bodies of her townspeople. Eventually, she opened her eyes and saw not the brown dust of the village of her home but the stark-white walls of a medical facility. This, too, she reasoned, must also be just a dream.

It was the rhythmic beeping of monitoring instruments she'd never seen before in her life that finally pulled her from her dazed state. At first, she tried to sit up but found that her whole body must have been restrained. She could not move a muscle below her neck, and even then her movements were limited. There was a tube in her throat, pushing and pulling cycled air into her lungs. She couldn't talk, or scream, or look around to figure out where she was.

Eventually, someone came to her. He was a smiling, bald man with glasses and an uncomfortable look around his eyes. He scribbled something on a clipboard, then pulled his glasses off to look her in the face. "I see, you're finally awake. We wondered if you would pull through after all the procedures," he said.

Beatrice's eyes went wide. *What procedures?* What had they done to her?

"Don't worry; we only did what was necessary to reclaim you. I understand this must all be confusing and scary. My title is Beastmaster, but my name is Dominick. I am a doctor, and my job is to help you transition into your new life in service of Prince Rholam, long may he reign," he continued calmly, glancing at the various instruments around her and checking them against the paper on the clipboard, "You were essentially dead when our soldiers found you. Thanks to my team, you will make a full recovery — and then some."

He flipped a switch, and the tube was yanked with

robotic precision from Beatrice's throat. She gagged and coughed, gasping for a moment as her throat constricted and her lungs tried to remember how to operate. She watched, drowning, as he pulled out a small black item with a glowing button on top and pressed it.

Suddenly, she found she could move. The feeling of her fingers and toes came to her with overwhelming sensitivity. She spasmed in the shock of quasi-painful overwhelm as her nerves tingled to life. Her lungs expanded, bringing with them a headrush of endorphins. On exhale, she let out a crying sob but found she still could not speak.

"I know," said Dominick, "you're grateful for the miracle of second life the Prince has granted you, blessed may he be."

She shook her head, feeling the blood rush to her cheeks as her insides turned with rage and guilt at making it out of the massacre alive.

"Ah, you're still upset," Dominick said, "well, you will be grateful in time. But now that you have recovered, we must send you off to the Academy for training."

Dominick pressed another button on the black remote control and Bea found herself standing up. It wasn't like she was being forced to; she suddenly felt like she wanted to stand. Endorphins hit her again as she obeyed the command that had nestled into her brain.

"We won't use that all the time, but we won't be engaging complete autopilot until we know we can trust you. Now, the next transit leaves the depot in a few minutes. What say we get you loaded up with the others?"

Chapter Five: Middle of Nowhere

Dominick directed her through the building. They went down several winding flights of stairs, which landed them outside. Waiting, presumably for Beatrice, was an automotive, powered by some magic unknowable to Beatrice. She had never seen anything like it in her tiny, dusty little town, where any automated machinery was rare, and electrics were taboo. It was docked at an elevated cement platform that loomed like a cave at the side of the building. Steam billowed around it, and a sharp blue light glowed beneath the white chassis.

Though she had slept the whole time she was in the medical facility, her body seemed to know how long it had been since she had seen the natural sky, down to the very second. After a moment in the cool, windy corridor, she caught the familiar scent of impending autumn. Truth fell upon her through the unfailing wheel of the year.

Dei's melted corpse had been left to rot, unburied, unmourned, not for days, but for months. All the while, Beatrice had merely slept. She wanted to weep, but biology refused her the catharsis, instead obeying and enjoying the commands offered by Dominick's remote control.

"You'll find good company in there," Dominick said as she stepped into the large tube-like vehicle and took her seat.

The door sealed behind her, and the long metal tube lurched forward. She felt her speech coming back now, slowly, like the sweltering heat of summer as it fades beneath the moon. As she waited for her mind to cool, she glanced around as far as her eyes and unmoving head would allow. There was not much to take in, so she focused on the woman with wide brown eyes seated across the car facing her.

The words formed in her mind first, coming slowly to her tongue. "What's your name?" She slurred. Her tongue was a sluggish weight, her voice foreign and distant.

"Eniko," the woman said quietly. Her voice was barely audible, even in the quiet cabin.

Nothing about Eniko seemed familiar. "Are you from West Desert?"

She shook her head. "No."

Beatrice could see dunes and dust passing quickly by through the window behind her, interspersed with grass and small outcroppings of cacti and Joshua trees. They were at the edges of West Desert, crossing into Southland. She had never been so far from home. The other passengers were silent. Some looked stoic, but most of the faces there were riddled with fear.

"Does anyone know where we're going?" Beatrice asked into the empty air.

"Nowhere." Said a voice from the front of the cab.

"The Academy," the red-haired person beside Bea said, in the sort of way that implies common knowledge.

Bea's head turned, and she found that she had some control. Enough control to swivel her head left and right. She looked hard at the other passenger, waiting for her questions to materialize on her tongue. It was slow going. When she finally opened her mouth to speak, the redhead interjected.

"I'm Pennian, by the way. Penn, for short. That side-effect does wear off, eventually."

"We weren't sure you'd be joining us," said the green-eyed woman to the right of Eniko. "Fieria," she said by way of introduction. "Those three over there are Alessan, Garresh, and Leodos. You're Beatrice, right?"

She nodded her head. "Just Bea. What's the Academy?"

Every face in the car grew pale and grave; except Penn's. Their face just got red and hot. "It's hell. Pure hell."

The transit took a sharp turn, and Bea's stomach rumbled. It was empty, of course, probably from being in a coma for so long. "Is there food there, at least?" Her half-hearted attempt at a joke fell flat, and everyone sat in strained silence. Bea stared out the window, allowing the passing scenery to envelop her tired mind.

It was nighttime when she woke up. The moon was bright and full, casting a silver glow through the sides of the transit, shading the forlorn passengers all in gray. Acid hunger gnawed at her insides, and her tongue was dry with thirst. No one else seemed to be asleep.

At first, she thought her ears were ringing, and maybe they were. The squeal of the transit slowing against inertia brought her fully into the moment. Eniko stared blankly out the window, silent tears streaking her cheek. There was the sound of a chain gate rolling open, and then the automotive carriage moved again with a rocking jostle and bump.

In the dusty dark, illuminated by the silver of the moon

and the transit's headlights on the fine sand, a sign read "N O W H E R E."

They had just passed it and pulled to another stop when the sides of the bus opened up. The passengers were greeted by orderlies wearing white smocks. Their faces were vacant, expressionless.

Out of nowhere, the disturbing buzz of a voice ordered them to stand – and they stood – and then disembark in an orderly fashion. Moving again, without the will or thought to do so, Bea lined up beside the other prisoners on the bus depot platform. The chilly night wind blew sand across her face. Her eyes burned, and she itched to wipe them, but of course, she could not move without the commands to do so.

She heard Dominick's voice well before she saw his bald head emerge from behind the crowd of orderlies. As she watched them part, she noticed they all moved like macabre rag dolls with lazy eyes. Whirring pistons shuffled them like lazy puppets to accommodate each other, heads cocked in uncomfortable positions, avian-like, to observe the newcomers.

"What does that sign say?" Dominick asked, pointing somewhere behind the bus. "The one you passed on your way in? Anyone?" He glanced around at them. "Let's not all scramble to be first, shall we? You're all so eager to please teacher. One at a time now...." It was all sarcasm. They hadn't moved a muscle – they couldn't possibly have moved an inch. "Ah yes, Beatrice. What does that sign say?"

Suddenly, she found she could speak. She felt not only able, but violently compelled to speak. She tried to hold it in, stuttering and biting her tongue until it bled, but the word flew out of her attached to gobbets of spit and iron. "Nowhere."

"Good, very good. You are in the heart of the middle of

nowhere. But don't look so glum! Sure, no one knows you are here. No one knows you're even alive. And if you manage to escape, you'll die before you reach civilization. But let's put a positive spin on that word nowhere. Think about it; envision the word in your mind. Break it into its component parts." He paused, taking a moment to walk down and back up the line of newcomers on the platform. The wind howled, shaking the transit car and the buildings with a rattling chorus that seemed to sing along with the way he said that godforsaken word.

Nowhere.

"It's made up of two words... now and here. You are now here, at the start of the rest of your life! The beginning of a second chance you never should have even received. And here, beginning now, like that word nowhere, we will be breaking you down into your component parts to build something better than you ever were before or ever could have been. So welcome, children, to Academy Nowhere, and congratulations!"

He grinned as he said it, and the orderlies began clapping in their uncanny way, digits and wrists flailing together to form bruises where they collided. Then, he swiveled on his heel, and Beatrice and her group followed like baby ducks, flanked by the mechanized meat puppets, into the silver-lit dim of the camp.

Chapter Six: Recruit

Beatrice's heart raced as they walked. It seemed there were some things even Dominick's magic machines couldn't control. But even as her heart and mind willed her to make a break for it, her body conformed, step-in-step to the movements of the others around her. Over the wooden platform, creaking and groaning as their feet struck it, downstairs and across an empty, dusty field. The platform was to their backs, bright white light shining like a star on the horizon. Ahead of them loomed a cement building, so many stories high Beatrice thought she would never be able to see the top of it.

The tin sign above the door read "ACADEMY." This building was lit with the same piercing white bright light as the other buildings scattered distantly around the compound. Beatrice had heard of this kind of electricity and even seen it used in the illegal traveling circus, *Contrabande Carnivale*. She'd been raised to know that if it was ever allowed again, this kind of power could revolutionize how people lived. But it was known across every region that Power Corrupts. This same life-altering technology had given rise to the wars that ended all things just a few generations ago.

But the people of Academy Nowhere seemed to use it flagrantly. The hum of electricity was in the air, and she could feel it in her hair, pinning her clothes to her with a tingling buzz. Everything about this place was *interdit*, as the circus performers would say. Forbidden. While unbelievably mortified, her curiosity was piqued. How had they made it work in the middle of the dead zones? How had they managed to hide it from the authorities?

The line came to a halt, and Dominick approached the front door of the Academy building. Then, something amazing happened. Beatrice watched as he pressed a button by the door, and a rectangle flickered to light with that same blue-white as her grandmother's old cellphone. It blinked, flashed, and then spoke in a honeyed voice.

"Biometric identification, please."

Dominick offered his palm to it, hovering just above the rectangle, blue-white light spilling out between the crooks of his fingers, and he replied. "Dominick Vandervein."

There was a reddish pulse of light around his fingers and then the sound of a lock clicking open.

"Welcome, Doctor Vandervein," the device said, flickering green before going dark again.

"Follow me," Dominick said as though they had a choice. The line continued forward again, and as she passed through, Beatrice could still see a faint gray glow where the device sat in the wall.

The inside of the building was lit with buzzing blue-green lanterns set into the ceiling every few feet. They followed Dominick up a flight of stairs, through a maze of corridors, and around a few corners. Beatrice tried to track where they were in relation to the front door, but it was no use. After five minutes of walking, she counted several double-backs, and everything looked exactly the same as everything else, so landmarking was impossible.

Finally, they entered a large open room where flickering white bars of light hung from the ceiling. Everything here was concrete – the ceiling, the walls, the floor. There were chips in the gray, suggestions that there had once been paint on the walls – walls which were now decorated with rust-tainted scratches from what looked like human fingernails. At the center of the room was a set of cement tables and benches.

"I bet you are all starving," said Dominick, "Have a seat then; let's get you some food after such a long, grueling journey. Warden?" He called, swiveling toward a dark doorway opposite the one they'd entered through.

Beatrice could smell something warm and foodlike wafting from that door, and when she turned to look, she found she had use of part of her body again.

"You'll be allowed to eat before your orientation to training," Dominick said, "The Warden will take it from here. Now, I know you're sad to see me go, maybe even a little bit afraid. But don't worry, I'll check in periodically to see how things are going." Dominick offered a wry grin. "Ah, here she is. Goodday, Warden!"

A large, broad woman entered, carrying a pot of something steaming. "Hi there, Doc! What a wonderful day to receive such a large shipment of new recruits!"

Dominick slammed his fist down on the table and growled, "Greet her, recruits."

"Hello, Warden!" The words compulsively tumbled out of their mouths in a haphazard jumble.

"By the end of all this, you will have come to view the

Warden as your new mother," Dominick said. "Sorry, Warden, they're not trained yet."

"No worries," she said, ladling slop onto the table in front of each individual recruit. "That's my job."

She poured a ladleful before Bea, and the hot stuff splashed on her face. It smelled... like food. Not good, not bad, but something of substance. Beatrice's stomach felt like Cerberus himself was nesting inside it. She watched as it dripped down the side of the table onto her lap and pooled toward the uneven divots toward the center of the table. She was hungry. She wanted to scoop it up into her mouth, slurp it off the dirty surface of the cement. She still could not move enough to do so.

The Warden finished pouring food onto the table and glanced over at Dominick. "Why aren't they eating?"

"Ah, yes," Dominick said, feigning forgetfulness.

Beatrice heard the small click of a button. Then she found herself suddenly, ravenously devouring the stuff, concrete pebbles, paint flakes, and all. She could hear the sounds of the others doing the same as she scooped and poured the tasteless stuff into her eagerly awaiting mouth, sucking her fingers dry like it was the best feast she'd ever had in her life.

It wasn't. In fact, as she continued to scrounge for droplets everywhere she possibly could, she found that it was not actually tasteless. The slop tasted like iron, like blood, like ash. It tasted like the explosion that killed Dei. It tasted like corpses and fire. But she could not stop eating it. Eventually, when there was nothing left on the table, she took to ripping at her smock – it was only now that she realized she was wearing a smock – to eat the pieces of fabric soaked in it.

Her stomach hurt, Cerberus screamed in rebellion as she tried to pile more and more and more into herself – until, finally, there was relief. She was restrained again, the silent click of Dominick's remote having reigned her into near immobility once more. But there are things even Dominick's remote can't control. Cerberus, who had nested in her cave-like gut, revolted. Everything she had taken from the table, from her smock, spilled out of her in heaves and hot waves until she was empty.

"Well, that's unfortunate," the Warden remarked.

"Ah, well. There's always at least one," Dominick said. "Shall I leave you to it then?"

"Yes, we clearly have much work to do," said the Warden.

The two shook hands, and Dominick departed with a wave, leaving the remote in the hands of the Warden.

"Alright, recruits, today is the first day of the rest of your life. You will hate me. My job is to make you hate me. But you will thank me, too, for this glorious chance to redeem yourselves by fighting – and dying – for the good of mankind. Now then, let's begin."

Chapter Seven: Reform

Beatrice tried to sleep against the surge and tide of wailing screams echoing from the main room at the center of their training hall. Every few minutes came the banging of hammers on the thick metal door to her dank, three-by-three cell. The orderlies never slept, devout in their religion of tormenting the recruits.

They took no pleasure from it; that was evident. But then again, they seemed to find no enjoyment in anything. Nor pain. They were mindless. Whenever one fell defective, it was killed and replaced, the body dragged to some unknown location to be repurposed into something else. Probably the slop they were sometimes allowed for dinner.

Echoes of pain and terror bounced around the claustrophobic space like fragments of a broken mirror. She tried to block them out and focused on her breathing, but it was no use. The fear was like a living thing inside her chest, clawing its way up her throat until she could barely breathe.

But fear, she was beginning to learn, could be overcome.

She closed her eyes and focused on the darkness behind her eyelids. In her mind's eye, she pictured herself in a different place, a place where there was nothing but peace and quiet and distance between her and the walls surrounding it. A place where she was safe and loved, and it smelled of dew-dropped grass, of Dei with a pan of fresh-baked bread, of her grandmother's dyed wool yarn.

In the weeks since arriving at Academy Nowhere, Bea had found herself subject to innumerable forms of psychological torture. It had become so that she'd built a castle in her mind, a place where she could sit back and watch through smudged windows as the things happening around her happened. But today would be a day of reckoning for Beatrice because today, she would not just be subject to the torment. No, she would be required to act. Act, or die. Beatrice would soon learn that the instinct to live is a powerful one.

Suddenly the door burst open, and light flooded in, shattering her brief respite. The metal cell door gaped like a greedy mouth, ready to swallow her whole. She stood against her will, bones and sinews vibrating with the tinny hum of Dominick's remote control. It had become her constant companion, that awful trill. It rang out above everything, a painful baseline screech that was impossible to ignore. She walked toward the threshold, marching to the beatless droning of the remote control's tune. No matter how hard she fought, no matter how defiant she was inside her mind, she could not keep from moving toward the place she'd come to dread.

"Is four weeks long enough to build a fortress?" She found herself asking out loud.

"What?" Asked Eniko, who was her partner for the next exercise.

"Nothing. I haven't slept."

"Hard to sleep when they're banging on the doors all

night!" Fieria said from across the room, emphasizing the last part with a smack of dry spit at the cement floor. The Warden, who stood at the end of the room in her perfectly pressed olive green uniform, gave a sardonic chuckle.

"How can you expect to survive hell and ascend to heaven if you can't let go of simple, imaginary limitations, like sleep?" She strode with mock thoughtfulness to the center of the room. "Now that you're paired up, it's time to begin the next training phase."

The group hit their knees with a slam, mouths clamped shut, eyes facing forward. Beatrice felt a sinking feeling in her gut. Today felt uncomfortably different from the previous weeks of mind-numbing torment.

"You are powerful beyond any measure you ever knew in your past." She paused in front of Fieria and Penn. She studied them momentarily, reaching a finger under Fieria's chin, tilting the green-eyed woman's head up slightly. Her voice lowered to a resonating growl. "Beyond the need for sleep or the craving of human food." She swiveled on her heel, releasing Fieria as she stepped to the middle of the group. "I have sufficiently deprived you to levels that would have killed a normal human. Now it's time to see how you fare in battle. Stand."

There was no remote control trill, yet Beatrice found herself rising. Penn also stood, face pale. Eniko crouched, cowering. Fieria and the rest of the class glowered at the two who stood.

The Warden practically purred, a grin splitting her face ear to ear. "Wonderful! These two are the most eager to survive – their fight will be a desperate one. Watch, class," she said, then waved Penn and Beatrice toward her at the group's center. "Now, the rules are simple. Rule number one: act, don't think. Rule number two: anything goes – as long as you're the winner. Rule number three: fight to the death." She patted them both on the shoulders and chuckled before backing off to the side and waving the others along with her. "This will be fun!"

Penn shifted into a fighting stance and looked placidly at Beatrice.

Beatrice put her hands up apologetically, palms facing Penn as she took a small step back, "I don't want to hurt you—"

Penn's fist landed Beatrice square in the jaw with a force that should have knocked her to the floor. But Beatrice was barely shaken, and before she had time to rein herself in, her foot kicked Penn into the wall behind her.

Penn slid to the ground, small bits of rubble falling from the fractures in the cinderblock wall behind her. The Warden cheered through flush cheeks, waving her fists in a crude imitation of a boxer.

"Penn, I'm so sorry," Beatrice said, pulling herself out of a mental haze. She approached her classmate, kneeling to pull her up.

Penn's eyes shot open, and the eager opponent swiped at Bea with her leg. "Big mistake."

Bea jumped the swipe, flipping backward in a feat of acrobatics she had never before attempted. Beatrice, the clumsy, unathletic farm girl who had never trained for fitness a day in her life, was backflipping away from her opponent.

She landed on the soles of her feet, shifting the inertia up the line of her body to heel-palm Penn, who had charged after her in a rage. Before she could even feel her hand connect, Bea's super body was already preparing for its next move.

As the two fought, matching each other in speed,

strength, and stamina, Beatrice felt herself slipping deep into a trance. Her body was humming, blood and oxygen filling her muscles and brain, endorphins racing with adrenaline to fill her with a delicious cloud of euphoric hyperawareness. From somewhere distant and gray, she recalled *rule number one: act, don't think.*

And then, *rule number two: anything goes – as long as you're the winner.*

Penn's blow landed her square in the chest, and she felt the power ripple through her. Bones might have shattered, bruises might have formed, but even as she fell, she felt nothing but the energy, the power, the rush. She felt her back hit concrete and lay there a moment, allowing her mind to drift up into the flickering fluorescent lights above.

And then a dark red cloud filled her vision. It was Penn, descending upon her like an eagle reaching for a snake, claws out, eyes sharp. Penn was swooping in for the kill. Talons wrapped around Bea's neck, and the world dimmed. She almost welcomed it.

Rule number three: fight to the death.

"No."

Beatrice felt her mouth form the word, though she could not hear it above the noise of the fight, the rushing of blood, the pounding of her eyes and head as she struggled to breathe.

"No."

Everything sharpened, everything dilated, and suddenly she was on top of Penn, pressing their face into the concrete. There was only one move to make from here. One move and she would win – she would survive. She wondered if she should feel something – remorse, maybe – at the thought of taking a life. She could sense the edge of it, like a half-remembered melody, but it never overtook her.

Maybe it was because Dominick had replaced her broken heart when he repaired her devastated body. Maybe it was because the Warden had ground them all down to their most primal, feral aspects. Maybe she had always been this way, cold and unfeeling.

All it took was a shift of her weight. A simple, almost imperceptible movement. She felt it, the crackling pop, the half-gasp, the sudden give like Penn's bones were made of jelly.

The Warden's voice came fuzzy to her ears as the hum of adrenaline began to wane. "Well done, Beatrice! Now then, who's next?"

Chapter Eight: East Desert

The Academy halls were silent. After what felt like months of training, nothing could phase the remaining recruits. They sat silently in their small, uncomfortable cells, sleepless, devoid of any feeling. Beatrice walked the halls of her mind palace, gazing over the structures she'd built there, passing by closed doors to rooms she'd locked and swore never again to open.

At the end of this particular hallway was a portrait of Dei, and on the table below it was a red candle that always burned and never melted. She wanted to feel something when she gazed at it, when she ran her fingers along the delicate lines of his cheekbones and lips. Sometimes, for a moment, she could feel the coarse edges of something within her. Anguish, perhaps, at his absence?

Alas, she was no longer bereft. Instead, she would find herself gazing into the candle flame, knowing that, though she was numb to so much, this little light was the spark that kept her moving forward. This was the thing that was keeping her alive. Not anger or grief, but the principal knowledge that those who had stolen her life from her were destined to pay the price. They would pay it with their lives, and she would be the one to exact that toll upon them.

She was drawn out of her meditation by the metallic *click* of their cell doors unlocking.

It was time.

Beatrice, Eniko, and Fieria stood at attention on one side of the room. Penn, Garresh, and Leodos mirrored them on the other side of the room. Alessan did not make it. Each of the remaining six had been revived and restored after various deaths during fatal training exercises. Their limits had been pushed, crossed, demolished. The words "fear" and "impossible" were no longer part of their vocabulary.

"Your first mission," said the Warden, "is simple. You will be deployed at a village outside of East Desert, on the edge of the Empty Zone. Your job is to corral the civilians and keep them concentrated toward the city's center. Tell them you are there to protect them from the coming invasion. If they resist, incapacitate them. If you must, shoot some to make an example, but we prefer most of them to stay alive."

The room was silent.

"Glad to see there are no objectors. You'll be accompanied by two other experienced squads. If you succeed in this exercise, you graduate from training. Now, go to the armory, grab your gear, and load up onto the Wraith. Dismissed."

Beatrice no longer noticed the ethereal humming that had once accompanied the Warden's orders. She moved, regardless of whether she heard it, knowing that following orders was the only way to stay alive, keep moving, and enact justice on those who had wronged her – and all of humanity.

She was the first to the armory, the first to stand in the dressing chamber and emerge clothed in the bulky armor plate. She was the first to grab her weapons – a laspistol, a bolter, a plasma rifle, and an electric baton – and take her seat in the silent plane. The Warden was pleased to see this, so while she and Beatrice were waiting for the others to load up, she pulled the recruit to the side.

"Beatrice," the Warden rarely used the recruits' names, "you have shown excellent initiative, survival skills, and, dare I say, leadership qualities. I will name you squad commander if your team succeeds in this mission."

Beatrice nodded in response. "I understand."

The Warden chuckled, patted Bea on the shoulder, and made her way to the front of the Wraith. The rest of the team boarded and strapped into their seats. "Now, remember, this is just like your training – except this time, it's real. This is the first time any of you will come across our enemy since you were extracted from your old lives." She paused as the Wraith engines rumbled to life and the pilots chattered to each other in the background.

"They are called the Behemoth. They feed on anguish and fear and the flowing blood of humankind. Hear me as I say this; if you forget your training, you will die. And in your death, you will betray your cause. Death, with its mixture of emotions, is prime fuel to them. As such, warriors dedicated to the death of the Behemoth – *heroes* – do not die. Only traitors succumb to the enemy. Is that understood?"

"Yes, Warden!" The team yelled above the Wraith engines, which were growing steadily louder.

The pilot turned and said something to the Warden, who nodded. "When you return triumphant, we will celebrate. Remember, the small part you play in today's operation will save more lives than you can imagine. Protect the weak, break the damned."

"Protect the weak! Break the damned!" cheered the team as the Warden deplaned and the craft lifted into the sky.

Beatrice, who had only been in the air as a part of training exercises, knew that a past version of herself would feel wonder at the astounding magic of flying machines that are invisible from the ground. But instead of looking out the hatch at the beauty of the world passing by, she flipped through the battle plan on the data chip installed in her helmet.

The instructions were clear.

At the red light, unbuckle and line up at the hatch. When the light flashes, jump out of the plane. Follow battlepak landing procedure. Arrive at the village on foot. Convene with the other squads. Corral the citizens. Wait for further instructions.

Soon enough, the light flickered red. The team stood and lined up. The light began to flash, and Beatrice checked each of them before she followed them out the doorless hatch, ensuring their battlepaks were secure. As the team leader, she was the last to take the leap.

She plummeted through the air, watching as the dusty gray of the dry lake bed sped by. The sky's blue lightened and then darkened as she passed through clouds. Finally, she saw the village coming up quickly and activated her landing jets.

The team touched down in a nearby clearing and made their way to the edge of town. They took cover behind some arid brush plants by the meetup coordinates and observed the place. They waited for some time. Too much time.

"I'm going in," said Penn.

"No!" Beatrice said, grabbing her arm. "No. We wait for

the other two squads. For now, we just watch. Be thinking about the best way to approach this."

"These people... they're so small. Were we ever that small? That weak?" Leodos asked.

"They're just like we used to be, Leo. Clueless. They will probably be terrified just to see us. They might think we're the enemy..." Fieria said.

"You have a point. Technology like ours is probably still contraband," Beatrice said pensively.

"Should we try to... I don't know, appear more human?" Garresh asked.

"No. We are not human, and we should not pretend to be," Beatrice said, her voice neutral and emotionless. "Our orders were to use what we have to corral them, bring them to the center of town. We wait until the other squads arrive."

They sat for an hour more, watching the people. Men, women, and children went about their daily lives, seemingly unaware of the impending danger. But Beatrice knew better. She could sense the growing electric charge in the air. In response, something -- not quite fear -- called the hair on the back of her neck to attention.

They're here, she thought to herself, *somewhere.*

Suddenly, there was a loud screeching sound and a missile's undeniable sizzling, whistling *kaboom!* Then, like a plague, the Behemoth descended upon the village.

They were not as Beatrice imagined they would be. When they attacked her old town, she only ever saw their ships, their weapons: the titanic mechanical monstrosity that manifested as if out of thin air and its buzzard companions zipping effortlessly through the smoke and wind. The elegant, intuitive crafts conjured to mind a machine-race of sorts. Perhaps some sort of bioengineered automaton army that vaguely resembled humankind. Maybe even something akin to Beatrice's own mechanized reincarnation.

As their name implied, the creatures were gigantic – easily twice the size of a man. They had large, leathery wings, and their bodies were covered in thick scales and sparse, coarse fur. Their mouths were filled with sharp teeth and long, barbed tails. After a moment, she registered the cries of men, women, and children as they were torn apart by the beasts or as lasers carved holes into their flesh.

How long had she been observing them?

"Are we too late?!" Penn asked into the vox.

"I don't know," Beatrice replied grimly, "the other squads haven't arrived yet."

Eniko opened fire on the creatures without warning, and some of her shots connected. One particularly gray Behemoth oozed maroon sludge from plasma rifle wounds beneath its shoulder.

"Cease fire!" Beatrice ordered, "You'll give away our position!"

"We can't just sit by and watch them get killed!" Eniko shouted into the vox.

"What the hell are we supposed to do here?" Fieria said. "Beatrice, you're in charge. Tell us what to do."

They were all looking at Beatrice now. After months of being remote-controlled, every thought and action so clearly ordered by the Warden or Dominick, now she had to make a decision. She broke radio protocol and sent a looped message out on all frequencies.

"All squads, this is Delta squad requesting backup. The Behemoth have arrived, and we are commencing migration of civilians from the east edge of town to the center of town."

Then she switched back to the third squad channel and

addressed her team. "Alright, we're going to start our part of the sweep and hope the other squads come in and close the gaps.

The team moved out of their hiding spot and went into the village. There, they found bodies – men, women, and children – strewn about the streets. It was quiet where they were, the Behemoth having moved further into town in pursuit of fresh death. The scene was one of utter carnage. Houses were destroyed, fires burned, and blood stained the ground.

"This is a massacre," Beatrice said grimly, "a damned massacre." Memories of her own town's destruction flashed through her mind. But she felt nothing with them but cold, clinical awareness that somehow she needed to turn this operation around.

Suddenly, she heard a noise coming from one of the houses. She motioned for the team to take cover and approached cautiously. She took two deep breaths, then effortlessly kicked down the door, swinging her rifle in a sweeping motion, finger on the trigger as she scanned. Finally, she saw what had made the noise: a woman huddled beneath a wooden table, her arms around two small children. The woman looked up at Beatrice with pleading eyes.

"Please," she begged, "don't kill us!"

"Ma'am, you need to get to the town center," Beatrice said, reaching out her hand.

The woman screamed and clutched the wailing children closer to her chest.

"Get up!" Beatrice yelled, throwing the table so hard against the wall that it shattered into splinters.

"What the hell is going on in there?" Garresh's voice rang out over the vox.

Beatrice grabbed the woman by the arm and dragged her out of the house. "We need to split up, these people won't listen to reason, and there is too much ground to cover. Go house to house, grab the ones you can, shoot the ones you can't."

"We were told to keep them alive, Bea," Eniko reasoned.

"You remember what the Warden said? About these things feeding on fear and death and flowing blood? They can't scare them if they're dead. They can't kill them if they're dead. Their blood will dry quickly in this sunbaked lake bed. Get them to the town center, or make sure the enemy can't use them. Those are my orders. Understood?"

"Yes, Ma'am!" The squad replied in unison.

"Move out."

The team moved quickly through the village, kicking down doors and rounding up people. They were efficient but not gentle. They had no time for that. The Behemoth were making quick work of the town.

Soon enough, the team could hear the screams of their victims echoing from just a street away. They were almost to the meeting spot at the town center, having sent scores of people out from their hiding places and out into the open of the town center. Blood trickled down the street gutters – some of it spilled by their own hands in the name of the cause.

The bright yellow of battlepak jets streaked through the growing cloud of dense smoke hovering over the town. Backup had arrived. Moments later, their comrades checked in over the radio. Beatrice and her crew reached the town center as the first complete transmission came through.

"Delta squad, this is Alpha. Do you copy?"

The sight was horrific. It was a bloodbath. She gestured to the others to surround the remaining civilians and defend them. "Copy," she said, blasting a behemoth with her bolter as it lept toward a crowd of cowering civilians.

"Stand down!" The deep voice crackled in her ear. She must have misheard. She fired again, and the beast hit the ground with a wet thud, mouth agape, inches from where she was holding the line.

"Repeat?"

"Stand. Down. Convene at the church."

Beatrice, confused, called to her troops. "We're being ordered to meet at that steeple to the east," she said.

"But the people... we can't leave them!" Leodos said.

"They'll die!" Cried Eniko as she sprayed a layer of fire at the barrage of Behemoth charging at them.

"We're here to follow orders, right?" Penn said, matter of fact.

"I don't know about you all, but I would rather graduate training today," Garresh concurred.

"Penn and Garresh are right; we're here to do a job. Our orders were to corral the citizens, then wait for instructions," Beatrice said.

"Delta, stand down, or you will be forcibly removed," the voice buzzed in her ear.

"Copy," Beatrice responded. Then, to her squad, "Let's go."

As they departed eastward, Beatrice knew, conceptually, that they were leaving these innocent people to die at the hands of the horrific Behemoth. Somewhere in the background, she could hear the heavy steps of a titanic metallic monstrosity. Who owned who? Did the Behemoth pilot the thing? Did it have a mind of its own? They fired their blue lasers, burning, melting, cauterizing everything they hit. The smoke and fire intensified, engulfing the sky.

They ran toward the church. Internally, she relived the

day the Behemoth descended on her old town. But instead of fear, or sorrow, or anguish, she only felt rage – smoothed by the calm of acceptance that there was nothing here she could possibly change on her own. She wondered if the others were reliving their own nightmarish original deaths.

They climbed the steeple and watched from the belfry as the people were fed to the Behemoth by the other two squads. Those who tried to leave were dragged back and tossed into the center of the carnage to be devoured by the hoard of Behemoth gathered there.

Chapter Nine: Killing Machine

"We weren't sent to save these people."

Fieria had finally spoken the words they were all thinking.

It had not even taken an hour for the corraled civilians to be devoured by the Behemoth, especially with the help of Alpha squad. Bravo squad had met up with Delta at the steeple and briefed them on their next moves.

"I wonder if our towns were bait, too," Beatrice said, louder than she'd meant to.

"Is there a problem, team leader Delta?" Bravo's team leader asked her.

"No," she replied. "Let's get going; it's almost time." It was clear now why the Warden wouldn't tell them the actual purpose for their presence in this sleepy town at the edge of the Empty Zone. It wouldn't be a real test if their loyalty wasn't pushed to what many of them would have considered a breaking point in their former lives.

"Remember, when the Cyclops reaches that point over there –" team leader Bravo gestured to a small mercantile building, " – you fire this hook into the hinge of its leg. Can anyone tell me what the dual purpose of this hook place-ment is?"

"It'll give the hook a solid grip–" said Penn

"And," Fieria interjected, "the machine will slow down because it has something stuck in its gears."

"Very good," Bravo 1 said. "And why is this dangerous?" Garresh raised his hand, and Bravo 1 gestured for him to answer.

" The hook will break under the pressure of the gears pushing down on it. The time we have to climb the wire is short."

"Short and?" Bravo 1 prompted.

"Unpredictable," Leodos said.

"Good. Good. Alright, it looks like we have time for two more questions before the target hits its mark. Your grap-plekit is hooked to the waist of your suit. Once your hook is attached to the target, what do you do?"

"Discharge the wire from the kit," Beatrice said.

"Good. And, of course, why aren't we just using our battlepaks to fly to and land on the target? Anyone?" Bravo 1 hadn't covered that in his brief. "It's simple. The Cyclops is clumsy, but its weapons are very effective – at range. The closer you are, the harder you are for it to attack. If you're *on* the Cyclops, it can't kick you off with-out, first, slowing down and, second, risking its balance. Speaking of, thar she blows!" Bravo 1 cheered, bracing himself as the ground shook with the Cyclops' mechanical steps.

"Harpoons at the ready!" He was clearly trying to make light of the situation. Delta squad all stood silently, fingers on grapplekit triggers. "Oh, come on. No one found that funny? Fine. Such a glum squad. We should rename you fuckers. Don't worry. You'll get the hang of things. Hopefully, today you'll see that it really isn't so bad once you're deep in it."

"Those people died," Fieria said, voice sounding haunted.

"They died to save others," Bravo 1 corrected her. "You have no idea what has been going on in this world and the fight we've been waging to ensure their sacrifices are not in vain. If you feel culpable for their deaths, think of this as your atonement. Now pay attention, or you'll miss your mark."

In moments, the Cyclops left foot smashed the mercantile, and the squad fired their grappling hooks. There was a terrible grinding sound as the machine struggled to take its next step. Sparks flew down at the squad of six as they swung, crash-landed against the metal appendage, and began their ascent. There was the sound of six distinct *pops* as they discharged their spent wires and clambered up the struggling metallic beast.

Penn was the first to enter the thing, dropping into an open ventilation hatch on the thing's lower torso. Fieria followed them inside. The pair made quick work of the creatures inside, which seemed to be smaller, more agile versions of the Behemoth. Leodos and Garresh were next, entering through a rolling door on the middle torso that Penn opened for them. Those four were to go and try to make the switchboards and mechanicals inside the thing's torso inoperable, killing any and all Behemoth they came across.

Beatrice and Eniko were tasked with entering the Cyclops' head and disabling the optical center there. They climbed using the magnetics on their suits, which made loud *vroc!* sounds with each arm and foot movement as they crawled ever upward. They crested the curve of the upper torso, passed over the shoulder joint, and found the head. It seemed large enough that it could comfortably fit all six of the squad, standing, sitting, or lying down – but there was no door.

The two pulled out their laspistols and stood out, horizontal as though the rules of the natural world did not apply to them, and fired into the metal. Eventually, they carved an opening. Beatrice braced her feet against the machine and pulled the metal sheet outward, and Eniko climbed inside.

Beatrice paused to look out over the city's carnage before ducking inside. It had become eerily quiet; instead of the screams that filled the air with the acrid smoke, there were only small wails, the sound of buildings collapsing under the weight of fire, and the dominating machine hum from the Cyclops. She was unprepared for what she would see in the optical center.

"Is that –?" She asked, not wanting to finish the sentence. In a past life, she would have been appalled.

"Yes," Eniko said, nodding, "I think it is."

A large glass tube that almost filled the space was at the center of the cybernetic chamber. The pair walked around it, peering into the brackish liquid that sloshed inside. The monstrosity within was some atrophied, horrific amalgamation of humanoid and Behemoth. Numerous tubes plugged into the body, some into the brain, others into the torso. There was some sort of fibrous cord attached to its spine.

From behind, it could have been human, but its profile bore a resemblance to the Behemoth. Its face, however, was unlike either of its progenitors. There were none of the typical landmarks of a human face nor the snout and fur of the Behemoth. Instead, buried in the naked, gray flesh of the too-round head was a single, massive eyeball.

It stared at them, expressionless. Knowing.

"We have to kill it," Beatrice said.

"Does it even know what it's doing?" Eniko asked, trying to reason with her teammate.

"We've been here too long already, and this thing needs to die." Beatrice aimed her weapon at the circuit board where all the tubes, cords, and wires convened.

"It's a living creature, Bea. It's like we once were...."

Beatrice whirled on Eniko. "These things killed our families, destroyed our homes. We should be dead because of these monsters, En! How can you suffer them to live? Seeing, knowing exactly the carnage they have wrought on humanity?"

Eniko's mouth clamped shut. There were noises below them; bolter fire, the scraping sounds of Behemoth being dragged to their deaths.

"The team is almost here. I will not tell them what you said to me just now. In the future, I suggest you keep thoughts like those to yourself," she said, punctuating her words with bolter fire as she destroyed the console that kept the mutant in the tank alive.

"No!" Eniko cried just as the rest of the squad joined them through a lower hatch. She huddled against the glass, staring into the eye of the creature as it suffocated and twitched.

"What the hell?" Garresh said.

"Eniko, step away from the glass. I'm going to put it out of its misery," Beatrice said.

"What's she doing?" Penn asked Beatrice.

"You can't kill it!" Eniko said, louder than any of them had ever heard her. She'd been so soft-spoken, even during the worst parts of training. But now...

"That thing, whatever it is, is part of the enemy, Eniko,"

Fieria tried to reason with her. "Literally a part of this killing machine."

"It's alive like we once were! You've lived a thousand deaths. We all have died so many times... this thing, it's pure. It's sheltered! It's never died... it's innocent, untainted!"

"Shit," Leodos said. "She's snapped."

"If she fucks this up, we all fail the test," Penn said, reloading their bolter with a new charger pack. "Eniko, step away from the glass, or I'll shoot you."

"No! You want to kill it, you have to kill me, too!"

"This isn't like in training, En," Leodos reasoned, "You'll die here, and you won't come back. You fail the test, you die, you're a traitor."

Eniko was silent for a moment. She let go of the glass, her shoulders going slack. Then, with a sad chuckle, she looked up at them. "Good."

"Fuck," Penn said, bolter wavering briefly in their grasp.

"I'm team leader," Beatrice said, placing a hand on Penn's bolter muzzle. "I'll do it."

Beatrice raised her gun. "Last chance, En. I am ordering you to stand down." The familiar hum enveloped her brain.

"Do it," Eniko said, "I should have been dead long, long ago."

Beatrice inhaled. Exhaled. Squeezed.

Chapter Ten: Dogfight

"Let's go," Beatrice said as the viscous green liquid poured from the shattered glass tube. The creature inside gave an unholy wail as it died, gasping, grasping, eye bulging and melting out of its socket as the outside air singed its veinous skin.

"Aren't you going to finish it off?" Garresh asked.

"They feed off our suffering, right?" Beatrice asked, firing off her grapplekit toward the belfry.

"Well, yes..." Garresh responded, puzzlement in his voice.

Eniko's dead body hung limp against Beatrice's, armor clanking together in an uncomfortable cacophony of discordant percussion. "Fair's fair," she said before dropping out of the open hatch Eniko had carved for her only minutes earlier.

"What happened?" Bravo 1 asked when she made it to the bell tower. It was clear by the tone of his voice that he probably knew exactly what had happened.

"She lost it," Beatrice said plainly as she unloaded the

body. "The others will be here shortly. What happens now?"

Bravo 1 reached out and touched her shoulder. "Look at me."

Beatrice looked up through her visor and his. Something stirred in her. It was sweet, gossamer, unidentifiable, gone. His golden gaze pulled her back to the moment.

"You did the right thing. Not everyone has what it takes to be a true warrior for our cause."

"I understand." She looked down at Eniko's corpse. "What a waste."

"It's all part of the test."

"You mean –?"

"I'm sure they knew she'd turn. There's almost always one."

Beatrice stared at the stiffening corpse at her feet. She'd seen Eniko like that before, but this time would be different. This time, they would not wake her up. Instead, they would extract the mechanical components from her body and repurpose her flesh into other things. Maybe she'd be reincarnated as an orderly. Maybe she'd be butchered up as nutrients for the next batch of recruits.

After a moment, Bravo 1 spoke. "Looks like the rest of your team is here. Let's get her packed into the Wraith and head home. Alpha squad is on cleanup duty."

"Do you think we passed?" Penn's voice pierced the silence. Their helmets canceled out the noise of the Wraith engines.

They were flying over the Empty Zone. There were no schematics of instructions to study, so Beatrice let herself watch out the open hatch.

Fieria replied, "Before today, I would say I don't care if we passed. But if I had to choose between killing Behemoth scum or facing down trials under the Warden's thumb again? I'd choose this every time."

"I think I actually had fun," Leodos said hesitantly.

"I'm glad someone else said it first," Garresh chuckled. The rest of the squad laughed.

"What about you, Bea?" Penn asked, landing a warm hand on her shoulder.

Beatrice pulled her eyes from the scenery and looked at the others. "It was an honor to lead you."

She was conflicted. They had led all those innocent people to slaughter at the town center, used them as bait. Eniko died. No, Eniko was killed. Beatrice *killed* Eniko.

The hum had yet to fade from her mind. It was probably a placebo, something pretend. Dominick was nowhere near their location. The Warden was back at the Academy. Who else could have pressed that remote button, commanded her to do such a thing?

She thought of her own finger on the trigger. Of Eniko's pleading eyes. She retreated to her mind palace and walked down Dei's hallway toward the red candle. There, on the wall, beside his portrait, was Eniko's. Below them, the flame seemed hotter, brighter. She took a pull of the fragrant scent of burning wax.

The hum shifted to a high-pitched scream. Beatrice was jostled out of her meditation by the sharp downward pitch of the Wraith's nose.

"Fuck!" Fieria struggled to tighten her seat straps.

"What's going on?" Beatrice yelled into the vox. She could see the pilots working frantically in the cockpit.

"Hell, Bea, did you fall asleep?" Garresh's voice was tinted with annoyance.

"I thought she was a little too quiet," Penn said sardonically.

"We're being chased by something!" Said Leodos finally, the first useful thing in the long anxious moments since Bea's sudden rousing.

Beatrice patched into the pilots' frequency – something team leaders could do – and listened.

Co-pilot: *I thought the fleet was further north!*

Pilot 1: *Looks like we made our bait a little too appealing. Three of them, hot on our tail.*

And then, an unfamiliar voice. *We're on our way, looks like they shot down the guys we sent to round them up.*

Co-pilot again: *For fuck's sake, hurry!*

Pilot 1: *Evasive maneuvers – and get one of the recruits on gun!*

Beatrice unclipped her seatbelt and buzzed into the vox. "We're not recruits anymore, we passed the test. I'm on it."

"What the hell are you doing, Bea?" Penn yelled, trying to pull Beatrice back into her seat. Beatrice pushed through her grasp and stalked toward the gunny seat at the side hatch. Her magnet boots made heavy thunks as she took her deliberate steps forward.

"They need help getting these fuckers off our tail. So that's what I'm going to do." The plane bounced high to dodge an enemy blast, and she sank low to the floor. She moved slowly on hands and knees to the seat, then pulled herself up and strapped in.

"No time to dally, Delta 1!" The co-pilot shouted.

"On it," Beatrice said.

With the press of a few buttons, the weapon arm swung out. She yanked on the lever to her right, and the seat swiveled her and the gun to face the targets. In her life before, she could never have conceived of doing something like this. Her shield screen lit up blue, and she shifted the turret to capture one of the enemy planes in the sight. After a few moments, the weapon locked on, and the target lit up red. She pressed the trigger, and the turret sprayed exploding lasrounds at the closest target.

The enemy plane dodged most of the rounds but took a few in the wing.

She heard Pilot 1 in her ear, "Finish it off!"

"Copy."

She slammed her fist down on the orb at the center of her console, and three heat-seeking missiles shot out from below her feet. The whole Wraith shuddered when they made impact with their two closest pursuers. Shrapnel flew, a piece of it sliced at her shield screen. The Wraith seemed undamaged otherwise.

"Two down," Beatrice said into the vox as she watched the two birds plummet toward the barren desert below. She glanced back up and saw their third pursuer slowing. "The third one must have caught some shrapnel. It's smoking pretty bad." On the horizon, she spotted three more aircraft approaching. "Where's backup?"

The co-pilot replied, "Nowhere close; seems they got caught in another dogfight on their way here."

"Looks like we have company."

"We're not meant for this kind of enemy contact. We're just a cargo plane!" the co-pilot shouted.

"Shut up and do your job," Pilot 1's words were punctuated by what sounded like a slap to the co-pilot's face. The co-pilot made no response.

"I only have three more missiles, but we should have enough lasrounds to take these guys out," Beatrice said.

"Do what you can, Delta 1. But we may have to ditch. We're leading them away from the Academy, but we're almost to the point of no return. Another thirty minutes of

this, and we'll run out of charge before we make it back."
Pilot 1 broadcast the statement to the entire squad.

"Could this all be part of the test?" Garresh's voice
buzzed in the vox. The pilots didn't respond.

"Garresh!" Leodos was incredulous.

"Test or not, I can tell you the enemy really is trying to
kill us," Beatrice said as she fired another round of blasts
from the turret. She'd be lying if the same thought hadn't
crossed her mind when the enemy fighters arrived.

"It's serious, test or not," Penn added. "Get your pack
ready to make the jump."

"We won't have to jump for another hour at least,"
Garresh said.

"Get ready anyway," Penn retorted.

There were four planes left, and Beatrice knew she
would run out of ammo before she took them all down.
They were tricky, nimble bastards, and she was only just
getting the hang of anticipating their maneuvers.

"Listen to Penn," Beatrice warned. "This is starting to
look like a losing battle." She unloaded the last of the
missiles and took down two more.

"Fuck," Garresh said.

"Fuck is right," Fieria replied.

And then it happened. Beatrice was overcome by something hot, explosive, jolting. And then she was falling,
scrambling to get into position, to right herself and employ
her battlepak.

Fuck.

Chapter Eleven: Empty Zone

Time and the world blurred by at impossible speeds as Beatrice spun and flailed like a ragdoll, trying desperately to correct her fall before it was too late.

A cacophony of vox transmissions muddled her brain.

Delta 1, do you copy?

Fuck, did she just–

Don't say it, Garresh!

We're losing altitude.

The right wing is compromised.

Shit, prepare for a crash landing.

Delta 1, hang on. If you can hear us, just hang on.

We'll come find you!

At last, she was steady. The ground was coming up fast. There would be no time to slow her ascent. It was now or never. She pressed the button on her battlepak and felt the snap of bones and popping of joints as the thrust of the battlepak broke hard against gravity. Debris showered her, slicing against her metal armor.

When it cleared, she looked up. A trail of smoke led

over the sun-bleached dunes. In the distance, she could hear the sound of the enemy planes and the Wraith's failing rotor.

Time to ditch.

It was Penn.

Delta 3, go!

Delta 4, go!

She listened to the count off as her squad jumped from the craft.

Just try to keep her steady.

Pilot 1's voice was placid against the co-pilot's frantic pleas.

I'm not ready to die!

And then they were out of range. Moments later, the unmistakable noise rang out across the sand. The Wraithe had run aground.

Her feet hit sand, and she rolled to soften her too-quick landing. She lay still when she stopped, assessing her body. She heard the enemy craft fly over her; it sounded like the remaining two had made it out of the fight. She played dead until the noise of their engines was long gone; then, it was time to triage.

Slowly, she sat up and slammed her hips back into their sockets. Up next, her shoulder. Once that was back in place, she ran a diagnostic on her suit. It indicated some internal damage to her body, some external damage to her armor. Her battlepak was busted from the unusual high-speed landing. She knew that as long as she kept the suit on, it would keep feeding her body medication to blunt the pain, promote healing, and ward off infection.

Even if she hadn't been injured, she knew the Empty Zone was hazardous to humans. It was toxic and unbearably hot. She could only imagine the excruciating death awaiting her if she removed her gear. She took a moment to center herself, and then it was time to move again. First, to the crash site. She needed to locate the others. Then, to the Academy.

The trek was surprisingly short. As she crested the final dune, she was met with devastation. Smoking shrapnel was strewn all across the burnt sand. Interspersed in the wreckage were the bodies of her teammates. She checked each for signs of life, to no avail. All of them could be revived if she could get them to the Academy in time. She dragged them and placed their backs against a sandstone ridge, feet pointing south. Hopefully, the shade here would preserve them.

Then, as she reached the bulk of the twisted metal, she noticed a trail of blood and footprints leading further into the Empty Zone.

"Hello?" she buzzed into the vox, "Pilot 1 do you copy?" No response.

The co-pilot lay twitching and dying on the ground. He looked in her direction with glazed eyes, but the shrapnel lodged in his skull seemed to have severed his ability to speak. His body was mangled, macerated by the crash and the sand. There were bends and breaks where solid bone should be. He was oozing fluids, and his skin had begun to boil in the toxic air. His bloody gargle mocked an attempt at words. She knew it could only be a plea. She knelt beside him and delivered him from his pain.

He'd died draped over the Wraithe's front console. Electricity sparked as she tossed his mushed carcass to the side. The console was obviously damaged, but she tried the radio anyway. The broadcast echoed in her helmet but was met with only static. It was a long shot – the Empty Zone was a wasteland, and the Academy was well out of range. The other areal team had been ambushed from what she'd heard before the crash. They had probably suffered a similar fate.

The sun was beginning its descent, and it was time to make a choice. She could head in the direction Pilot 1 had apparently gone, or she could start the journey toward the Academy. Her friends could be saved if she made it to Academy in time. At first glance, the answer seemed simple. Academy was probably a few days' trek away, assuming she walked nonstop. But then, another thought crossed her mind.

The pilot was clearly injured, so why hadn't he gone in the direction of the Academy? If anyone knew of a closer safehouse, a place with a medical facility and supplies, it would be him. She looked back to the bodies of her squad.

"I'll be back, guys," she said into the vox, knowing it fell on ears that might never hear again. And then she left.

As the hunt ensued, the trail thinned. Shadows stretched long and blue over the golden dunes, and she hoped she was getting closer. Perhaps the pilot would stop to rest. Perhaps he'd build a fire, and she could help him get to the facility quicker. But then, as though he had ceased to exist on the spot, the pilot's footprints and blood droplets vanished from the sand.

"What the hell?" She said out loud. Puzzled, she glanced around. The air was growing gray with dusk. She was running out of time.

And then, the sand that usually gave way so gently beneath her metal shoes became stubborn. Her soles had traction, and her footsteps made a hollow sound that echoed solemnly off the walls of sand surrounding her. Could this be the break she was searching for?

She glanced down, and the cool breeze whisked the sand in gentle swirls over the hard metal surface. She knelt quietly beside the door and lifted it upward to reveal a cellar. A dim glow spilled from the opening, illuminating her suit and the sand in a ghostly bluish-white. There was a slick of blood along the doorframe. Almost imperceptible was the din of urgent conversation somewhere deep in the bunker. It sounded serious. Hushed. She thought she perceived the words "amputate" and "concussion" mixed in with the swarm of word soup bouncing off the bare metal walls of the interior.

It seems the Empty Zone is not so empty after all.

The door had been too easy to open – why hadn't they bothered to lock it up after the injured pilot came inside? Quietly, she lowered herself down and closed the hatch above her. More blood decorated the floor in thick droplets. A spatter of crimson on the wall bespoke a dying man's coughing gasps for air.

A row of monitors to her right depicted mortifying scenes of villagers being herded to their certain doom at the hands of the Behemoth. Her stomach turned.

Beatrice knew she should leave. No one was meant to know this place existed. And if they found her? A new recruit just barely out of training lurking the halls of a bunker buried in the forbidden sands of the Empty Zone? That would certainly mean the end of her life.

And why should she stay at those odds? Beatrice knew she could not find salvation for her team in a place like this. The pilot would be lucky if he made it out of there alive.

But she also knew she would never be able to slake her thirst to know more, to understand the true intentions of these people she was indentured to – and more importantly, to maybe find a way to free herself from the grasp of the technology her body had been forced to obey upon its rebirth.

Determined to learn all she could before she made a run for her life, Beatrice slunk into the shadows and began to search.

Chapter Twelve: A Mind of Her Own

The bunker was massive, filled with a labyrinth of offices, locked rooms, filing cabinets, and theaters filled with computer monitors and untold forbidden technology. She could not possibly hope to weed through all of it in a lifetime, let alone the sparse minutes she had left before it would be time to leave.

Many times, small groups of workers would pass by, some laughing, some serious, all moving with a clear purpose, all holding documents and tablets. As Beatrice hid from them – sometimes in impossibly plain sight – she noticed something peculiar about the people here. None of them were dressed for protection against the toxic atmosphere of the Empty Zone.

Was the bunker some kind of safe zone? Or was the Empty Zone's fatal air a lie, also? The further in she went, the more questions multiplied in her mind. Her most burning question?

Who are all these people, and whom do they work for?

None of them wore masks, ventilators, or even protective gloves. But they did all wear an insignia on their shoulder. It was a red lightning bolt encircled in a wreath of red thistle, all on a gray background. The symbol wasn't just on the people; it was everywhere – on the walls, on the rugs, on the documents, and on every piece of equipment.

Suddenly, an alarm began to blare. Klaxons and flashing red lights filled the air, and Beatrice knew she'd been found out. Quickly, she began making her way out of the maze of cubicles and winding corridors, back toward the hatch she dropped in through.

But then she realized something. They probably knew where she'd come in if they already knew she was there. And if they knew where the breach was, they'd probably be waiting for her there. Which meant that her capture was inevitable. So instead of walking into the trap, she turned around and headed deeper into the bunker.

As she skulked in the shadows, collecting as much intel as her memory system could hold, the klaxons silenced, and an announcement blared through the speakers.

"Delta 1, this is Pilot 1. I told them who you are. I told them you are a victim of the crash, like me. Come to the room where you entered the bunker, and they will tend to your wounds. There is no need to hide. Do as I say, and you will not be harmed."

Lies!

It had to be a trap. The Academy could make many more like her with ease. She was disposable, and she'd already seen too much. The klaxons resumed, and she burrowed deeper in.

After a short time, the pilot's voice echoed through the halls again.

"Delta 1, you are disobeying direct orders from a superior. Do not forget, we know how to control you. I have the remote right here."

She felt a sharp tingle dance up her spine, and the familiar hum sang in the back of her head.

No!

"You know what you must do. Stop digging and go to the rendezvous point. The more you see, the worse it will be for you."

No.

The hum increased, and she clenched her teeth, pushing one foot and then the next in the opposite direction of the command. Her vision blurred with effort as she trudged ahead, as though through a sandstorm. She yanked her helmet off and gasped at the cool, stale air. She threw it to the ground, and it rolled to a stop at a dark blue wall. The labyrinth had ended, and there was a door ahead of her. She knew she was on the edge of something, and whatever it was must lay beyond this door at the farthest end of the bunker.

Her vision faded to black, and she retreated to her mind palace. She focused on the red candle, flame flickering, and dancing. Each out-breath felt like her last one, almost extinguishing the very thing keeping her alive. Her limbs tingled, and she felt the siren song hum, severing her soul from her body. She looked at the photo of Dei in her mind, its image warped, melting with the beads of sweat that drenched her face and hair.

Twitching fingers grasped the door locking wheel before her. She weakly pulled, but the mechanism did not budge. In a last effort of desperation, she took a deep, shaking breath and flung herself at the heavy metal door. It was already unlocked and, though heavy, gave way against the full weight of her armored, metallically reinforced body. Exhausted, she sprawled on the floor as the door closed behind her with a clang. The hum faded to low-level background noise, and she dipped briefly into sleep.

After a few moments, her faculties returned to her. Her vision cleared, and her muscles, which had all been clenched tight in spasmodic resistance, relaxed. Weakened but regaining her breath, she stood and surveyed the room.

I can't believe I did it... I... I resisted.

It was a big room with a high ceiling. To the left was a lit fireplace framed by a couch and two chairs. The tables beside the seating arrangements were stacked high with books. To the left was a wall of bookcases and filing cabinets. Straight ahead was a wide desk that faced the door she'd thrown herself through. It was covered with sprawling maps and plans. Behind the desk was a tall back chair.

"Now let's figure out what this is all about...." She muttered to herself as she stepped toward the desk.

And then the chair swiveled.

"Well, now, that was quite the entrance, Beatrice."

Her stomach dropped.

"You shouldn't be here, but I think you know that."

"How–?"

"We've alerted the Academy of your escape. Dominick will be here soon, and I doubt he'll be very happy."

Fatigue coursed through her body to her fingertips. She dropped to her knees, eyes glossy as her gaze raked over the face of the person before her.

"What's wrong?" The man asked, "You look like you've seen a ghost."

"You were dead...." Her mouth was dry.

"So were you." He leaned nonchalantly against his desk.

"You work for them...?" Her voice sounded distant.

"So do you." There was no compassion in his voice.

"Not by choice."

His gaze sharpened to a glare. "You made the wrong choice, then."

"They're the reason our town died. The reason we –"

"Everything we do here has a purpose, Beatrice. Every one of us who was brought back was brought back for a reason."

"They're using the laypeople as fodder for those... those... monstrosities!"

He shook his head. "If only you knew, Beatrice. But I see now that I couldn't possibly get through to you when you're like this. It looks like you might need some retraining." He pressed a button on the intercom on his desk. "She's in my office."

"No, Dei, please... just listen to me. We can get out of here together. We can leave!"

Dei smiled down at her. It was a haunted smile that did not reach his empty eyes. "No one leaves this place, Beatrice."

Chapter Thirteen: A Heart, After All

Dominick's footsteps clicked behind Beatrice in their familiar, uncanny timbre, "Now, what have we here? A warrior seeking asylum? Or, perhaps, a spy?" He bent at the waist, so his eyes were level with hers where she knelt. The hum squirmed at the back of her brain, commanding her to look at him. She successfully resisted, but she caught his smirk in her periphery. "Hm. Precocious." He stood with a flourish of his white lab coat and moved to stand between her and Hodei. Beatrice studied the carpet.

"What is your assessment, Doc?" Hodei said casually.

"She can be repaired. But we need to move her out of here, and I don't think she's receptive to orders at this time."

Beatrice's pulse picked up. Had he just admitted they could not control her?

"I know something that might help," Dei said, then gestured to someone behind Beatrice, "bring in Maddeus."

"I'm not sure that's a good idea," Dominick said.

Dei waved him off, "I think I know her well enough."

"Very well," Dominick ceded with a delicate bow of his bald head.

Maddeus? She felt herself weaken at the name – her brother's name. She almost stood, almost turned toward the door, almost ran out there to greet him, to take him and run. Maddeus was supposed to be dead – but a lot of things were supposed to be true, and she could not trust anything she thought she knew.

"I think you'll like this little surprise, sweetheart." Dei's voice dipped sickly sweet. How many nights had she longed to hear his voice? Now she could barely contain her revulsion at the husk of her best friend as he stood before her. She wanted to weep. She wanted to scream. She did nothing.

Behind her came the sound of soft, padded footsteps, and she knew. She'd known that gait since he was a little boy taking his first steps. It was Maddeus. It was her brother. Between the steps was the clink of an ankle chain. He was cuffed. She felt his warmth as he passed behind her; the familiar scent of home filled her nostrils.

"Beatrice, is that you?" His voice, once soft and warm, now sounded tired and aged. She looked up at him, squinting against the yellow lights to see his scarred face. He was starving. His clothes were rags.

She broke.

With a speed that surprised even herself, she swept the leg of the guard escorting him and pulled their laspistol out of its holster. She shot the guard dead, then fired two more rounds to take out the pair standing at the door. The scent of burning flesh filled the room as she shot down the other two guards on either side of Hodei and Dominick. None of them saw it coming.

They all hit the floor, and she leveled the pistol at Hodei. "You should have stayed dead the first time."

"You don't want to kill me, Beatrice. You love me, remember?"

"Shut up."

Dei raised his hands in proverbial surrender. "Okay, so you shoot me. And then what?"

"I can just bring him back again, Beatrice," Dominick said.

The pistol flashed gold in the yellow light when she whipped it to the side and shot a hole straight through Dominick's hand. He dropped to the ground, screaming and stuttering. "Now you can't."

She pivoted back to Hodei, who looked down at Dominick with little more than disdain. "You know, I'm not his biggest fan either."

"What... the... fuck!" Dominick finally managed.

Hodei stood up from his perch atop the desk and took a few steps toward Beatrice and Maddeus. "Are you sure you want to do this? Killing someone in my position... that's a pretty big risk to take against your life."

"Maddeus, get behind me," Beatrice said. Her brother did as he was told. She kept the gun trained on Hodei, then told Maddeus, "Spread your legs as wide as they'll go."

"What?"

"Just do it."

"Alright..." As soon as his legs were apart, she slammed the heel of her boot down on the middle of the ankle chain. The links broke with a clash.

"Gather all their guns," she told him, "and shut him up," she gestured to Dominick, who was weeping on the floor. Maddeus did not question her this time.

"You'll never get out of here, especially if you kill me," Dei said.

"You don't know what I am capable of," she growled.

"Don't I? Who do you think sent you to the Academy? Who do you think made you Team Leader?"

Despite herself, Beatrice felt her aim waver. Maddeus hit Dominick over the head with a pistol. Blood soaked the floor where the doctor lay. "No. I don't trust a word out of your mouth, Hodei," she spat.

"Alright. Kill me then."

The hum was screaming now, having grown more intense with every contrary move of her body and mind.

She studied his face, her heart breaking all over again. She stepped closer, and pushed the gun to his temple. She towered over him in her power armor. He still looked like the boy he'd been, young and free. She felt the tears begin to well, and she shuddered a sigh. Breathless, she stooped and leaned her face against his. Her tears soiled their cheeks as she moved to kiss him one last time.

"I never got to say goodbye..." her voice cracked.

"Everyone is born alone; everyone dies alone," he said.

If she closed her eyes, she could imagine they were lying out in the sand beneath the full moon, musing about a life they had not yet begun to taste in its fullness. "I promised to take us out of that town... I wish we'd stayed."

"Bea... If you're going to do it, then do it."

"If I left now, would you come with me?"

"There is only one way out of here, remember?"

She squeezed the trigger.

The candle blew out.

Epilogue

Sunrise blossomed through pink-petal clouds, and the morning air was quiet and sweet. Glimmers of glass glinted and winked from between grains of sand as she trudged toward the distant, looming tower. The peaks of its minarets glowed gold against the bright sky. The hum tugged at the back of her mind, but she willed it away.

"We're almost there, Mad," Beatrice said. Her brother was unconscious, slung over her broad, bare shoulders like a wounded lamb. They'd been wandering for three days, presumably unpursued, and Maddeus had slept for most of that time. His body had not been prepared for such an arduous journey through the Empty Zone.

She scratched the scab of someone else's dried blood off her chin. They'd left the bunker a blood bath – no survivors. Her power armor had run out of juice by the end of the second day, and her wounds ached as she pushed on, day and night. She did not rest.

Her tablet still worked and held all the intel she'd collected from the bunker. She used it sparingly, pulling it out only to verify that she was still on track to reach their destination. In all her searching that fateful night, one document had stood out the most.

It was a map – unassuming at first. A digital copy of some old drawings of the land before the world had ended. But there, right by the edge, was a depiction of a castle flanked by a crest. Below the crest was a string of words in an unfamiliar dialect which roughly translated to the following:

Haven for the seeker. Refuge for the runner. Peace for the weary. Salvation for the damned.

The sun was near setting by the time they reached the gates. Maddeus awoke as they passed beneath the shadow of the imposing structure.

"How can a place as beautiful as this exist in a world as cruel as ours?" He asked through cracked lips.

"I don't know," Beatrice replied, lowering him to the ground, "but let me do the talking."

"It's probably abandoned," Maddeus said, ambling weakly toward the well near the entrance. After a moment, he gasped. "This well has... it looks like clean water in here!" Desperate, he reached for the hanging bucket.

"Wait!" Beatrice said, her voice hitting harsh against the warm sand. Maddeus dropped the bucket and ducked on instinct. "It could be a trap."

Eyes wide with fear, Maddeus peered back at her from behind the curve of the well. He was shaking like a leaf.

"Ah, Mad, I'm sorry. I didn't mean to–"

Maddeus shook his head, tears rolling down his dirty cheeks from unblinking eyes.

"What is it?"

Maddeus pointed a shaking finger to the gate behind her.

Slowly, Beatrice turned.

END.

About the Story, an Afterword by the Author

Content Warnings

It is important to note that the original concept for this story was based on my own traumatic experiences and personal struggles.

The reader is warned that this section of the book discusses topics of personal trauma related to sex and sexuality, purity culture, religion and high control environments, emotional and physical and sexual abuse, and mind-control, as well as co-morbid concepts such as systemic oppression, suicide, classism, and sexism.

The reader is advised to use discretion, read with care, and be mindful of their limits and needs.

How it All Began

The idea for *Academy Nowhere* came to me in a dream in 2014. It was vastly different in its original form, with its first draft coming in at about 50,000 words long, and its sequel reaching approximately 20,000 words before I ran out of steam. I shelved the project in 2015 and it sat in a forgotten folder, untouched, for seven years.

When I began writing this story, I was making my first attempt at college, pursuing a degree in elementary and early childhood education at College of Southern Nevada. Most of my writing in this story took place on a covered balcony at the east campus — usually on a Tuesday, since my best friend, Ty Jacobo, and I were carpooling to classes. Because of our class schedules, our Tuesdays started at eight in the morning, and usually did not end until almost nine o'clock at night. Between classes, we either would nap in the vacant hallways or take advantage of the free wifi to update our content — writing, review swaps, covers, etc. — in our preferred Figment communities.

Looking back, this was a hard time for both of us, and Tuesdays offered us something of a respite. We each had our independent struggles, and it was nice to have that reliability of at least one day per week where we would have a chance to bounce ideas off one another, offer kindness and support, and find ourselves beholden to no-one but our class schedules and our creative whims. I will forever be grateful for the hours we spent together during those years just reading, writing, laughing, crying, napping, eating, plotting our revenge, and, very occasionally, actually doing schoolwork.

Ty Jacobo and I met in 2011 and I am proud to say our friendship has lasted to this day. Neither of us finished those particular degrees at CSN, and our life paths significantly diverged in 2016. Ultimately, and separately, we both wound up running our own little hybrid-indie publishing operations. We both still joyfully collaborate with each other on creative projects and hang out digitally through video calls and online chatting, and I am grateful to still call Ty my friend.

Thank you, dear reader, for indulging my digression. Let's get back to 2014, when Dream Story came to me in, well, a dream.

From 2013-2015, I found myself deep in the throes of a violently abusive relationship. My escapism took the form of a frantic attempt at MilWordY, which would later burn me out on writing for three whole years. Much of what I wrote during that time is reflective of the abuse I was going through, as I was struggling to process the sexual and physical violence thrust on me by this one person. Simultaneously, I was instinctually beginning to detangle myself from my toxic and cultish "nondenominational" white-Christian Evangelical upbringing *and* grappling with my gender identity under the restrictive cis-heteronormative culture I felt beholden to.

Needless to say, most of what I produced at that time is utterly unusable in its original form. Much of it is nonsensical, poorly written, and laden with thinly veiled trauma dumps. The only beta reader who made it most of the way through the original draft of *Academy Nowhere* was tablo.io author T Van Santana, with whom I have unfortunately lost touch but whose science fiction works I highly recommend.

Now, let's talk about the journey of creating and revising this story. It's been a healing and restorative process to go back and reclaim ideas that came to me in that difficult and confusing time.

The Original Concept

First, I want to show you a collage of some things I created during this time period that are directly related to this story. Formatting can sometimes be weird, so if there's no image on this page, check the next one. Alt text is included for those with screen readers.

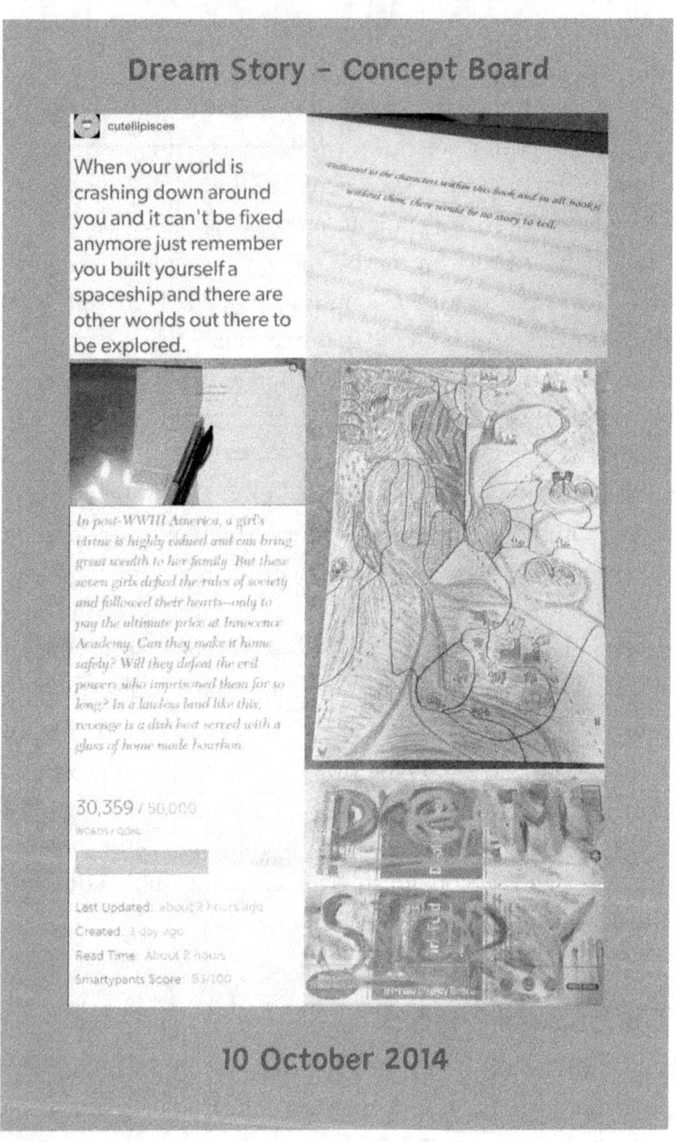

Now, let's talk about it.

World-building is my favorite part of bringing a story to life. I often use multimedia approaches to help myself alchemize my ideas into words. In this case, I got a tri-fold poster board — the card board kind we Millennials used for school presentations — and drew out a map with markers and colored pencils. It took about six hours to make. The closed flaps can be seen in the bottom right of the image, where I hand-painted the title "Dream Story" in blue and purple acrylic paint.

I wanted to depict a post-apocalyptic dystopia that had reverted back to the feudal system, slavery, and indentured servitude. In the original version of this story, the nation-state is called "Desert." It's located in the southwestern United States after WWIII. As you can see from the map in the collage, the nation is divided up by industry and class, and the blurb indicates the location where Bea ends up was originally called "Innocence Academy." Incidentally, *Innocence Academy* was one of the options I considered for the original version's title.

From that same blurb, you can also see that the premise is different — the original was based around punishing people who deviate from the intense purity culture, including our main character. The blurb makes it evident that she survives the horrors thrust upon her by authorities, then pursues revenge against them. The blurb does not discuss the other compelling elements of the story, such as discoveries that Bea makes about what the world outside her small community is actually like; ultimately she discovers that her entire way of life was a sham.

Allow me to elaborate. Lower class citizens live their lives with some very specific beliefs, which are spoon-fed to them by the hyper-subtle propaganda that surrounds them from birth. Some of these concepts remained in the final story.

- Electronic technology is incapable of functioning due to a special WWIII weapon deployed over 50 years ago. *Author note: this is an untruth designed to keep non-elite citizens from forming connections to the outside world.*
- Electronic technology is the reason why WWIII broke out. *Author note: this is an untruth designed to keep non-elite citizens afraid of progress.*
- Electronic technology should be destroyed if found, otherwise it may one day broadcast dangerous mind-control technology that will lead to mass genocide and war. *Author note: this is an untruth designed to keep non-elite citizens in the dark about the true causes of The Disaster, and event I never fleshed out but wanted to address in the sequel.*
- There is a global shortage of food and resources, thus making poverty a virtue. *Author note: this is an untruth designed to keep non-elite citizens weak and impoverished while elite citizens needlessly hoard resources for themselves.*
- There are less than 500,000 people left on planet Earth, and it's impossible for any of the "countries" they've formed to reach each other, due to mass destruction of the planet. The severely damaged areas are called "dead zones." *Author note: this is untrue. I did not decide how many people were left on Earth after The Disaster, but the planet is not so far damaged*

that people can't travel or contact each other between continents or across oceans. Dead zones are actually exclusive to this particular dystopian society, and are actually just secret areas where the military and government operations take place. Labeling them as dangerous or useless wastelands keeps the uninformed away from top secret operations.

- There is no overarching government running "Desert," nor is there an official military associated with "Desert." There are only small, municipal governments and general social tenets that guide the society's functions. *Author note: this is an untruth designed to keep dissatisfied citizens from finding someone to unite and rally against. The idea is not exclusive to the lower classes — even most of the elite believe this to be true. No visible oppressor + the weight of widely-accepted social rules = a nearly-cemented status quo.*

- Sexual virginity is more precious than anything else and those who lose theirs preemptively or don't conform to the cis-heteronormative social rules about sex should be severely punished if not killed. *Author note: this is untrue and its only use is to keep funneling more people into the lower classes and to keep society's anger or frustration focused on the imaginary "social denigration" and "moral corruption" of their society instead of an oppressor. Also serves to eradicate non-conformants by both murder and suicide.*

These concepts make up the basis of a "Desert" citizen's framework. It's unfair and cruel and a decent example of a dystopian fascist society with some underlying conspiratorial factors built in. It also sort of lines up with some real-world antisemitic conspiracy theories I grew up believing to be true — such as the "Deep State," or the purported evils of philanthropist and Nazi-occupation survivor George Soros. The virginity thing obviously comes from purity culture and the sense of life-and-death that evolves in the hearts of many who grow up under that kind of belief system.

Above all else, the original story was intended to be a commentary on purity culture and what it might look like if pushed to extremes. It was a reflection of how I felt being raised in that sort of environment while simultaneously having that "purity" ripped away from me, and being shamed for being interested in sexual intimacy before, during, and after that occurred. In the original story, Innocence Academy was a conversion camp where a sort of born-again "neovirginity" was forced on the prisoners by way of creating a sexual aversion through violent and forceful means. Conversion therapy, fear mongering, slut-shaming, and abstinence-only education are all tactics still used by Christian organizations today to further purity culture.

While, generally, no one is being raped or electrocuted for the sake of preserving purity (as were the main characters in the original story) there is a sort of mental rape that takes place for those of us who have endured such Christian methods. As children we're told that our own virginity is not even ours to give away. As we grow, we're taught that seemingly innocuous, normal human things are actually scary evil temptations to our brothers in Christ — regardless of how old they are, or how old we are. As our adult interests develop, we're taught to suppress and hide those very things that might make intimate connection possible — be it a gender identity, a sexual orientation, a kink, or a desire to explore our own bodies. In that sense, our internal innocence is stolen from us and the sweet innocence of butterflies and firsts are rebranded as satanic.

I think Bea's shattered perspective was a reflection of my own at the time. I was beginning the arduous tasks of reframing the loaded language I'd learned growing up (I call it Evangelical Vernacular), learning how to use logic and reason despite seemingly innate thought-stopping techniques, and realizing that the "secular" world was vastly different to what I had been told it was my entire life.

- Bea and I both realized that purity culture was a means to oppress and subjugate, not to uplift and reward.
- Bea learned that technology was *very commonly* in use outside of her community and so had to learn how to navigate it in order to live in society, despite her ingrained fear that it would bring danger and destruction to herself and those around her. Likewise, I had to learn to speak secular without being afraid I'd go to hell and drag others down with me.
- Bea discovered that there wasn't a shortage of food and resources, nor was there a dearth of human connection in the outside world. I eventually discovered joy, kindness, and friendship in a world I'd once believed was a barren wasteland dedicated to evil and suffering; as it urns out, "secular" folk aren't all depressed and angry and starving and dying

and terrible. Generally, it seems most of us are pretty dang okay.

So. Let's talk about how *Academy Nowhere* ended up.

The End Result

You're reading this afterword, so I'm assuming you've read the story already. That means *spoilers ahead*.

The version of *Academy Nowhere* that made it to print obviously underwent some serious rewrites. I first picked the story back up at the beginning of 2023, nearly ten years after its inception. The original had never made it successfully through a single beta-read, and with good reason, so I, with open eyes and a very fuzzy memory, undertook the task of re-reading the beast and deciding what, if anything, to do with it. It was a monumental undertaking, considering the state of that original draft and the state of my mind when I had written it.

Ultimately, most of it got scrapped. I threw out all but around 7,000 words of story, which I would then pick through for usable parts. I kept most of the main and secondary characters, kept the town where it started, kept the mysterious lair in the desert and idea of some creepy reformation center in the middle of nowhere... and not much else.

On my read-through, I realized that if I really wanted to use any part of Bea's story, above all else I needed to drop the whole purity culture thing and prioritize repurposing the academy. I knew I wanted to keep a small element of romance, but I wanted it to be unconventional and confusing. I opted not to make her family out to be accessories to the villains, and introduced a secondary, red-herring type of big-bad... *the Behemoth.*

The Behemoth were also the product of a dream from a few years back. I knew I wanted to integrate them into some kind of story, but I hadn't figured out where they fit in until I decided to repurpose the academy as a tool for military indoctrination and troop radicalization. The Behemoth are a foil to the secret government, initially being presented as the ultimate bad guys but quickly falling into second place as Bea uncovers the distasteful truths of her nation.

Because I thrive on gray areas, Bea never learns the full story behind the Behemoth or the government, and the reader is left guessing as to just how involved Dei was in the attack on their home town. We never find out what happens to Bea after she and her brother reach the Fortress. I've considered doing a sequel, or carrying the story through as a novel-length production, or even generating a prequel that chronicles the cataclysmic events that led to the current state of the world. At the moment, I am very satisfied with where the story landed.

In the shadowed aftermath of global cataclysm, Beatrice navigates a treacherous landscape of lost dreams, enduring friendship, and unspoken love. As she's thrust into the cold halls of the enigmatic "Academy Nowhere," an oppressive force seeks to mold her into an obedient soldier. With each chapter, Beatrice's spirit is tested against the stark backdrop of dystopian science fiction, heart-wrenching connections, and chilling moral quandaries. From desperate battles against monstrous foes to confrontations with the very essence of her identity, she is faced with choices that challenge the core of her humanity. As mysteries unravel and allegiances shift, will Beatrice find the strength to defy her fate and reclaim her destiny? Dive into a world where the boundaries blur between survival and sacrifice, and where hope teeters on the knife-edge of despair.

That's the blurb for the final project. The reader will probably note that this blurb is *much* better than the original, and I certainly agree.

Closing Statement

So why am I telling you all of this? What was the point of this 2,800-something word essay at the end of a book that's less than 18,000 words long?

The reader may be wondering... *Could this have been an email?*

Sure. Email, blog post, whatever. But that wouldn't be nearly as special, I think. This is the type of story that's best told person to person, and since I can't be there with you right now to tell it, this is the next-best option. I trust that this story will find the right people, the ones who need it or want it or are looking for something to tell them whatever it is you're getting from reading this right now.

Here's the gist: I want to impart to you, special friend who has miraculously come into possession of this exclusive printed piece, that *Academy Nowhere*, a my grimdark short story, is a very personal project with raw beginnings. It, like myself and like my craft, has evolved over the decade to become something almost entirely new. I think that's a beautiful testament to the ability of people to *heal* from traumas, *learn* from mistakes, and *grow* in whatever ways we need to thrive.

<u>And to creatives, specifically:</u> Some things are meant just for us. Other things need to sit in a drawer while they — and we — mature into something our readers can actually digest. Still, other things are risky, raw, dangerous... and worth sharing anyway.

I will leave you with one last sentiment, which I hope to be known for by the time I reach two hundred years of age.

All art is garbage.

That is to say, all things we create will be loved and despised by others — even our used tissues, that pair of socks with ten holes in them, and that novel we spent three years working on.

There will always be at least one person to admire your work, and at least one person who wants to light it on fire and scatter the ashes over the Mariana Trench.

Sometimes, both of those people are you.

Thank you for your time.

-Zak Lettercast

P.S. February 3rd is Green Apple Day. No, I don't mean the day of service. I mean the day that Ty Jacobo and I accidentally traveled to a dimension where green apples did not exist.

Celebrate by sending your friends and family images and art of green apples, making them thirsty for the flesh of a fresh, crisp, green apple. Bonus points if it's a Tuesday.

On the 4th, indulge in a luxurious green apple and think of the things and people in your life that you would miss if you were accidentally teleported to a parallel universe where they didn't exist.

Finally, express your gratitude in whatever way feels appropriate.

-Zak Lettercast

About the Author

Zak Lettercast is a queer multi-genre author and poet. Grant writer by day, world-builder by night, Lettercast has several fiction and nonfiction publications under xyr belt. Xe also spearheaded the VeryGood Collaboration anthology project from 2021 to 2024.

Xe finds joy in eloquent turns of phrase and expansive universes, and xe firmly believes in the power of art and words to inspire personal growth and social change. Lettercast is nonbinary and thinks neopronouns are incredibly fun.

You can subscribe to xyr mailing list here by going to https://ilettercast.com/subscribe and following the prompts.

facebook.com/ilettercast
instagram.com/ilettercast

Also By Zak Lettercast

Gravity [3]

After three hundred years in hypersleep, Brian awakens on the *Vorena* at some unfathomable distance from Earth. Despite all the time and distance that has passed, it feels like mere days since he's left behind the loves of his life and the only home he's ever known. He finds some respite from his grief in the form of cryptic distraction when is thrust into a mission alongside fellow crewmates Yvain and Nydia.

Their task: to unravel the mysteries of an alien message that might hold the key to humanity's future.

As they navigate the complexities of their mission amid the confines of the *Vorena*, an unexpected bond begins to form among them. Surrounded by the serene passing of infinite stars, their camaraderie blossoms into a deep, unexpected affection. But just as they begin to come to terms with their feelings, a life-threatening health scare leaves one of them fighting for survival. Will they band together, or will their blossoming romance be torn apart?

Gravity [3] is a tale of love and resilience, of three souls intertwined by fate and choice in the cold vastness of space and dark nights of the soul. It is a story about three people united by true love and a shared destiny among the stars.

Desert Castle

Dive into a riveting blend of fantasy, horror, and mystery, where every chapter is a doorway to forbidden knowledge and age-old secrets. Will Caerulean and his allies stand firm, or will they be consumed by the shadows they fight? Discover a tale where destiny isn't preordained but forged through choices and alliances.

From whimsical castle bordellos to etherial battles of the celestial kind, the narrative explores power dynamics, desire, and the balance between fantasy and reality. With elements of gothic romance, erotic fiction, mythology, and psychological thriller, the story keeps readers engaged with its tantalizing interactions and forbidden secrets.

Arachnapocalypse! The Anthology

Arachnapocalypse! The Anthology is a collection of riveting tales about life in a grimdark post-apocalyptic world riddled with otherworldly horrors. Follow the adventures of people just trying to stay alive in the chaos that is *Arachnapocalypse!*

The *Arachnapocalypse!* universe spans a significant chunk of time, starting when the Arachnids landed on Earth in 2018. Some of humanity manages to survive the arrival of the giant flying techno-spiders from space, but just barely. As the humans rebuild, new and wild dangers arise. This alternate timeline devolves into higher and higher stakes as the stories progress; from a body-possessing space-fungus to unhinged scientists to super-soldiers and even spider-loving cultists, there is something in this anthology for anyone who enjoys an excellent grimdark or sci-fi horror read!

It Feeds

"The place was drawing him in, and he knew it. Carefully, he unsheathed his sword and wrapped the rosary around the hilt. The threshold was in sight, and its portcullis was wide open..."

Follow Llewis's harrowing journey into the heart of the Tower, where he vows to vanquish the warp-beast that slew his battalion's leader.

It Feeds is a short, gritty horror that will fuel your nightmares for years to come and leave you wanting more.

400-Year Frost

Imagine being one of the last humans allowed to escape Earth in her death throes, and then, hundreds of years into your journey across space, you are the sole survivor of your space-craft's collision with a literal star. That's Pete Garrison's story, and his drive to survive is so tremendous that he winds up making an impossible discovery...